Edward Locke Tomlin

Rhymelets

Edward Locke Tomlin

Rhymelets

ISBN/EAN: 9783337260965

Printed in Europe, USA, Canada, Australia, Japan

Cover: Foto ©Andreas Hilbeck / pixelio.de

More available books at **www.hansebooks.com**

RHYMELETS

PRINTED BY

SPOTTISWOODE AND CO., NEW-STREET SQUARE

LONDON

R H Y M E L E T S

BY

EDWARD LOCKE TOMLIN

LONDON

LONGMANS, GREEN, AND CO.

AND NEW YORK : 15 EAST 16th STREET

1891

Dedication

TO MY WIFE

While the Harrow pædagogue
Tried my soaring brain to clog
In the commentators' fog,

I was often far away
Where the Muses held their sway,
Penning many an idle lay.

In the Oxford lecture-room,
Theory, critic, axiom,
Seemed like phantasms to loom,

While my fancy loved to be,
In a sea-shell by the sea,
Venus there to comfort me.

Education, then complete
(Love's and Muses' alphabet),
Found me kneeling at your feet ;

In memory of happy times,
Listen. to my youthful chimes,
Take this bunch of early rhymes.

CONTENTS

THE END OF DEATH

DEATH built himself an adamantine hall,
  Moated in the dim sea that moats the world.
From the grim battlements his seneschal
  A blood-red flag unfurled.

The walls were hung with silence, and no sound
  Clanged from the pavement 'neath his iron heels,
Light only flickered from the courtyard ground,
  Ponded with fiery weels.

Death raised his sceptre like a lurid star ;
  Before his ebon throne obedience
On bended knee bowed his three henchmen, War,
  Famine, and Pestilence.

B

Beside him sat a woman, robed and plumed
  In leprous white, pallid, white haired, white pearled
About her pearl-white throat, her eyes consumed
  With flames that sear the world.

Her name Decay.   Death loved her, she that still
  Indissolubly bound to Life as spouse
Had power with many a welcome guest to fill
  His hope-abandoned house.

Then came there one who danced before the throne
  With rhythmic steps and dreamy cadences,
Her eyes like to a lustrous opal stone
  Seen through long eyelashes.

Lashes whose lengths were shot with rainbow gleams,
  Like sunlight shed on seaweed in the deep ;
These are the magic crystals known as dreams,
  Tears from the eyes of Sleep !

But Death arose and cursed her, for that she
  Brought souls to him on iridescent wing
In painless wise, her opiate set them free,
  And robbed him of his sting.

Forthright another, like a summer storm,
   With summer lightning eyes that flashed and failed
Whirled her lithe limbs in movement multiform
   Of beauty half unveiled,

Then sank and slowly raised her rounded arms,
   Pleading, a syren with no soul within.
Death looked and laughed upon her wanton charms.
   His well-beloved Sin.

Yet he arose and cursed her: ' Ay, cajole
   Full many a one to love and cling to thee,
But each is thine, thine only, till his soul
   Sicken, and longs for me.'

Then cursed he his three henchmen, for that they
   Made Death seem welcome and a little thing;
Fain would he, like a purring tiger, play
   With what his cublings bring.

' Thou, ruthless War, for all thy score of slain,
   Slain souls that come, their hands imbued with blood,
Hast let the hope of glory dull their pain
   And nerve their lustihood.

' Famine, what hurts it to the wasting sense
 To lose its being at the last extreme?
Too quick thine arrows pierce them, Pestilence,
 No time left to blaspheme.

' They rob me of my terrors : some the priest
 With prayer and crucifix and hope of heaven after,
Some opiates soothe, some the materialist
 With " Nothing is hereafter."

' But thou, thou art more gracious, O my queen !
 Mine, mine for ever when Life himself be dead ;
I love to see them linger, the has-been
 Haunting their dying bed.

' First fruits of russet locks are thine, Decay ;
 The first dry wrinkle 'neath a love-sick eye,
The first sharp pain, the first hair turning grey,
 Remind them they must die.

' ' Thy poison falls upon them drop by drop,
 As minute after minute saps their strength
Beauty and manhood fade, and, fading, stop
 To weep Life's little length.

'To me their tears are nectar, wine their gall,
  Their every sigh makes music in my ears ;
All thanks, my queen, from birth to burial
  Thou fillest them with fears.'

Black in black armour, kingly in king's guise,
  Death sat, and the white woman on him turned.
She sighed, and from the furnace of her eyes,
  There fell a spark that burned,

That seared, and left pearl-white upon the black
  A growing stain, while a shrill shudder went
Like a sharp sword sheer through him, front to back,
  With stab omnipotent.

For the first time light shone upon the blind,
  Uprose a rustle from the silent stones ;
The dead were laughing, like dry leaves in wind,
  The laughter shook their bones.

Sin swooned, and Sleep, with pleading eyes, besought
  Rest, rest eternal, for the restless dead ;
The black king gazed, with passion overwrought,
  While still the white wound bled,

As the white woman leaned on him, and, faint
   With the last effort of her failing breath,
Infected him and filled him with her taint—
   Decay had ended Death.

Sudden, like desert sandstorms spiralled high,
   The fiery weels went whirling up the night,
Then spread in softened splendour o'er the sky.
   Till the dark dead knew light,

And the dumb dead found speech, as the loud sound
   Of stone that crashed, struck spark, and roofs that
      flared,
Crackled, and left them roofless and unbound,
   While New Life's trumpet blared.

AT KARNAK

Speak, if ye be not dead, O old-world gods !
Speak, if ye be not dumb !   We know you not ;
Our fathers and our grandsires knew you not !
But once there lived a race of men who knew,
Who hearkened and obeyed your word revealed,
As we obey a revelation now.
Speak ! for I feel your presence.   Who has wrought
Such ruin mid your temples ?   Who has laid·
A hand so heavy on these ponderous piles
That they have crashed and fallen, or where they stand
Are but a ruin-wrinkled, shapeless mass
Of colourless, inanimate, void rock ?
Perchance within this hundred-columned hall,
God dryads by these godlike trunks of stone,
Greatness in greatness ye yet hide yourselves,
Aye ! all Olympus.   'Tis a lordly spot
For gods, or ghosts of gods, to dream of prayer.

AT KARNAK

CHORUS OF DEITIES

There is no God but Time,
   We bow ! we bow !
The darkness of his wings
   Is round us now.
Our halls were high, Time sent
   Earthquake and sand and sun ;
We linger, bowed and bent,
      Undone ! undone !

SEMICHORUS

Time was old when we were young,
   Time is young now we are old,
Every creed in every tongue
   Passeth as a tale is told.
      Undone ! undone !

Isis

Goddess, I, of secret rites,
  Beauty of Earth's early prime,
Offerings from a thousand fights
  Made my mysteries sublime,
I have fallen from my heights,
  Blighted by the breath of Time.
            Undone ! undone !

Venus

Goddess, I, who scorned her veil
  Scorned her secrets, showed the truth,
Taught the heart of man to fail
  Before my beauty and my youth ;
Taught him love, and taught him pleasure,
  Taught him roseate, amorous rhyme,
Rhymeless Time has blurred the measure,
  Love is killed by loveless Time.
            Undone ! undone !

AT KARNAK

ZEUS

I once gods and men kept under,
  Ruled alone o'er earth and heaven,
With the terror of my thunder,
  With the lashings of my levin.
Time has reft man of his wonder,
  Reft my gods of power sublime,
Seized my sceptre broke asunder.
  I must bow to Time.
              Undone ! undone !

CHORUS

Time was old when we were young,
  Time is young now we are old,
Every creed in every tongue
  Passeth as a tale is told.
              Undone ! undone !

O.N THE NILE

SPREAD the sail and ship the oar.
Loose us from the sunburnt shore,
        Ha ! Yalesah !
Father Nile will bear us on
Through his summer 'neath the sun,
        Ha ! Yalesah !
Father Nile is slowly sinking,
Earth and sun his streams are drinking ;
But his heart, far in the hills,
Year by year his bosom fills,
Raising richness out of dearth -
'Tis the pulse-beat of the earth
        Ha ! Yalesah !
Forth the oars and furl the sail ;
''Tis not that the breezes fail,
But the zephyrs are afraid
Of the ripple they have made,

And the stately solemn palm
Loves his image in the calm,
        Ha ! Yalesah !
Peace and calm ; we leave behind
All the passions of the mind,
Learn from Nature to be kind,
        Ha ! Yalesah !
Let us drift while drift we may,
Live to-morrow as to-day ;
Drift, until we drift away
To the shadow land for aye,
        Ha ! Yalesah !
Put the oars into the skiff,
Bear me forth to yonder cliff,
Lay me in the peaceful gloom
Of some Pharaoh's empty tomb,
There my requiem shall be,
In slow chaunted cadency,
        Ha ! Yalesah !

AT BIARRITZ

The wave that breaks upon the shore to-day
Is voiceful of the mighty yesterday,
　It broke upon and buried stone by stone—
Lemuria and Atlantis, where are they?

And where shall we be when the laboured stone
Of our proud palaces is idly thrown,
　In rounded pebbles by the sounding sea
On future shores of continents unknown?

Death hath no sting, no victory hath the grave,
For the imagination of the brave,
　Who know they only lose their sudden form,
And break as breaks on shore a broken wave.

Their Mother Ocean takes them back again :
We pass as the wave passes ; we are fain
   Of those unruffled depths from whence we sprang
Though the rude touch of earth be passing pain.

Some on a soft and silvery sand are spent,
Some driven high and hoar on rocks are rent,
   Some curling crash, and cease in midmost course.
All, sometime, in one common end are blent.

'Tween the dim past beyond our memory's range.
And the dim shore ahead, we feel it strange
   To wander as the winds list ; but we know
There is no death, no ceasing, only change.

SANSARA

THE sky above seems darker—further, sadder ;
  The vortex of existence whirleth fast,
Unto the day sufficient. 'Are we madder
  Than the mad past ? '

No sea flower but possession kills its beauty,
  No earth flower can live on in plucked bereavement,
No joy of sense, ambition, even duty,
  Survives achievement.

Our impotent dominion over matter
  But brings to light the powers of decay ;
Wisdom's or weapon's war, the printed chatter
  That rule to-day

To-morrow are not amid newer newness,
　　Though blood and brain their influence inspired ;
We chase a phantom, cannot capture trueness,
　　The hunter's tired.

Religion, wealth, or politics may beckon,
　　They offer peace, or place, or potent gold;
While soul and sense upon the bargain reckon,
　　The frame grows old.

We wrestle our environment to weaken,
　　We fight to loose the bandage from our eyes ;
Or earth's success or heaven's be our beacon,
　　The struggler dies.

The vortex deepens as the centuries send us
　　Faster and faster through the mad world's fight.
Shall the last word as the first word befriend us ?
　　' Let there be light.'

AFTER READING 'RE-INCARNATION'

THERE is no God who the tired soul befriendeth?
  No devil to stifle life at man's behest?
There must be new life when the old life endeth?
  There is no rest?

What! We must suffer a new agony of being,
  The dying rattle be a birthday breath ;
When the grave closes, it is not a freeing,
  There is no death !

A sea plunge in a momentary madness,
  A bullet in some baptism of fire,
They are no opiates for eternal sadness !
  Vain the desire

To anchor on the tideway everlasting,
  Where the soul must voyage evermore,
Chained to life by fetters of God's casting,
  There is no shore !

An eternity of ever old to-morrows?
   No delirium of devils could outvie
Such a horrible conception of new sorrows
   That cannot die.

Better the hells and haloes of the clergy,
   Though priests may lie and miracles deceive,
Better to kneel and chaunt a long liturgy,
   Say, ' I believe.'

Better to live with hopes of nearer heaven,
   To join the Church's chorus of ' I know,'
If to believe can exoterically leaven
   The earth life dough.

Best to march bravely in the path of virtue,
   Spend and be spent outside all dogma's pale,
Pass when the hour comes where no God shall hurt you,
   Behind the Veil.

Somewhere, sometime, in the infinite hereafter,
   The prodigal sad soul shall cease to roam,
Shall find surcease of tears, surcease of laughter,
   Shall enter home.

FAITH, HOPE, LOVE

FAITH'S

Like a lost iceberg in a southern sea,
Majestically melting. Where we see
    It diamond hard with hues of Paradise
To-day, how soon no trace of it shall be?

Hope,

Silent and pure as light mid man-made din,
Glistens above the battlefields of sin,
    Like a white bird against a thunderstorm.
The herald of a heritage to win.

Love,

When the spent sun his latest beam has shed.
When sea and land are travailing of their dead,
    Shall be the password to a higher sphere
Of Godhood from a manhood perfected.

LIFE IS ENOUGH

Life is enough.   At its innocent beginning
  All the world is sunshine, and for joy thereof
Tears pass away as mists of the morning thinning,
          Life is enough !

When the days darken and all the ways are rough,
  Work on, the web of Life is worth the spinning,
Though crossed the woof with warp of harsher stuff.

Thy duty done, the goal is near the winning,
  Dread not a devil's ' All hail,' a god's rebuff,
If there be life in the grave despite our sinning,
          Life is enough.

TO OMAR KHAYYAM

Omar, the fragrance of the ruby wine,
The scent of all the roses that were thine,
   Outlive the memory of thine empty glass,
And with the new-bloomed Orient entwine.

Yet all the teachings of thy roseate verse
Can nought redeem us from the western curse
   Of doing, doing, in rash recklessness,
So but we may put money in our purse.

Wisdom, awake in the reposeful East,
Disdainful of the greatest, as the least,
   Brow-bound with fillets of forgetfulness,
Lets loose her saffron robe with them that feast.

Thou gazedst in her eyes, but couldst not tell
If heaven looked back on thee from them or hell ;
   Knew'st not if she were saint or sorceress ;
So there were love, wine, roses, it was well.

So were it now, had we thy grace to see
The nothingness to us of what's to be,
    The utter nothingness of what has been,
That more men know the more they disagree.

Could we but learn from thee how it were best
With pillowed head on some still lovely breast
    No care, no thought, no fear of the unseen,
Rose-crowned to sink into the perfect rest.

FIRENZE

ONE spring when buds were full in Fiesole,
 The vernal breath of genius passed and stirred
Into strong notes of ardent sympathy
 The heart-strings of the herd.

Upon the surface of the smoothen rock
 The youthful Giotto lay ; there deftly drew he
With sharpened flint the firstling of his flock
 That ravished Cimabue.

From palace unto palace where they shone,
 From cloister unto cloister, still sublime,
His frescoes face us, though their hues are gone,
 Blurred by the breath of time.

His shepherd tower the old world's wonders ended ;
 Imperishably beautiful it stands,
With hues of many a marble softly blended,
 As from a painter's hands.

Firenze! what a heritage is thine!
  Massed marble forms, by master minds enchanted,
Tower and dome and palace, line on line,
  Thy peerless founders planted.

And still poor Arno laps with lips of love
  The feet of bridge and palace, church and wall ;
The deep blue spreads from hill to hill above
  A glorious funeral pall.

For over thee the modern death-in-life,
  That sees no beauty in the poet's song,
That heeds not when creates the sculptor's knife
  The beautiful, the strong,

That looks on Art as something almost mad,
  And reverences beauty only when
A money value for it can be had,
  Has fogged thee in its fen.

Some chose the tools of Art, but more of War,
  In the young time when every pulse beat high,
When every man to his own self made law,
  To carve his mark or die.

They wrought for work's sake and for love of deeds ;
  Untrammelled of the reasons, their bright brains,
Their souls, were in their finger tips, their creeds
  Arteried in their veins.

Where the frowned front of Strozzi rears his scars,
  Ear-ringed with iron, many a party feud
Broke high below the massive window-bars
  In steel foam flecked with blood.

Firenze ! all the anguish Angelo
  Wrought in his Dawn and Twilight, Night and Day,
Has laid upon thee since that time of woe
  Thou lost thy liberty.

What words of scorn would not thy Dante breathe
  On slavish moderns, who have placed the best
Of beauty, art, and handcraft far beneath
  Foul Medicean interest.

Sleep on, great souls, great city, till there come
  A truer knowledge 'tis not time to wake ;
Sleep on ! nor heed the modern bee-hive hum,
  Till the new idols break !

NUBIA

' LAND of gold,'
Thy name of old,
Lords of thee carved it on lordly shrines ;
The yellow spoil
Of sifted soil
The Pharaohs sought from the distant mines.

Their tale is told,
And gone their gold,
Thine still is the labour, thine still the toil ;
An acre of wheat
For a town to eat,
And meagre the pittance of date and oil.

For the sound of the grinding is low,
Only the ceaseless moan,
Where the pitchers dip, dip,
In the weary flood below,

To pour from a weary lip,
In a ceaseless weary flow,
  Creak, moan, creak, groan,
Their dole from the flood below
  To make the gold to grow.

Golden crops to foster thy life,
Golden fruits of a yearly strife,
Yearly strife with the golden sand,
Sterile robe of a sterile land !

Past the wild rush of the cataract dividing,
  Past the black basalt gleaming in the sun,
Past the dull roar of rock and river chiding,
  Enter we the land whose golden days are done.

Here where the hillside hems the desert distance,
  Here where the herbage narrows to the Nile,
Free from the strain and struggle of resistance,
  Anchor we in stillness by fair Phile's isle.

Sheer to the bank a ruinous repletion,
  Carved in the sunshine, painted in the flood,
Great with the columned beauty of the Grecian,
  Holy of Holies, solemn solitude !

'By him who sleeps in Phile!'
　　Supremest oath of all,
'By him who rests in Phile!'
　　Dread oath beyond recall!
Dread god, thy rest is broken,
　　Thy deathless death is dead,
Rude feet thy sleep have spoken,
　　Thy power, thy priests, are dead!

Beyond, with gloomy terror beautiful,
Far in the mountain's midmost caverned cool,
　　The kingly builder sits beside his gods
To guard the sculptured vast of Ipsambul.

Without, four giants on a giant throne
Kept watch in fourfold majesty alone,
　　Till by-and-bye the earthquake passed, and wrote
His Mene Tekel Peres on the stone.

From temple unto temple, king and god
Trod peoples under as red wine is trod;
　　Till one by one Time took and shook their halls,
And overset them, crying Ichabod.

Golden land,
Golden sand,
Beauty of river and rock and shrine !
And the lesson taught
To live for nought
But to-day and nature still are thine.

A VISION AT TOURS

I WANDERED on through busy streets,
  Where shop-fronts glisten with modern ware
Wondrous wares, though each man one meets
  Passes neglectful and hardly stares.
    Is there nothing but earth thereunder?
Where are the abbots, knights, and friars,
  Who jostled and feasted in old Touraine?
They planted grapes, these are but briars—
  These modern anthills of greed and gain !
    Where are all the dead, I wonder?

Was that an earthquake passed ?   It shook
  And shivered the plate-glass, drew the nails
That held those gaudy signs ; and look !
  Has twisted awry the tramway rails,
    And set the houses arocking ;
The stones are heaving, chimneys reel,
  Walls wave like tapestry to and fro,

Split like thunder clouds, peal on peal,
  In lightning ruin, while close below
    There echoes a ghostly knocking.

Wondrous white from her darksome tomb,
  Under the tower of old Touraine,
Luitgarde arises athwart the gloom,
  She that was wife to stout Charlemagne,
    Around her a motley thronging.
Scowling Louis, Tristran l'Hermite,
  Prowl again in the light of to-day,
While smileless Henry turns to greet
  The glorious abbot of Turpenay.
    Hark ! the bells above ding-donging !

Ten million gnomes run to and fro,
  Each with a stone like a hump on his back ;
Over each other like ants they go,
  Tumble and scramble, and in their track
    Rise in their stony vastness
St. Martin's church of silver sheen,
  And Henry's castle with frowning wall,
While, like a network in between,
  Street and tower and banqueting hall
    Complete the ancient fastness.

The air is full with sounds of eld,
    Echoes the lay of the troubadour,
Rings the lance on the blazoned shield ;
    There 's a stifled groan, *peine forte et dure,*
        A wretch in the dungeon is crushing,
While soft and low from church and shrine
    Rolleth the chaunt of priest and choir ;
Soldiers are quarrelling over the wine,
    There 's a clash of swords, a smell of fire,
        And the whiz of arrows rushing.

.

'Tis well to wake from good old days
    (*Pace* Balzac, thank God they are dead),
For e'en the ruddy firewood blaze,
    The cheerful gleam as I raise my head
        Can hardly dispel the sight there ;
Beware of mixing in old Touraine
    With red-backed Murray ' Contes Drolatiques,'
For sure as castles are built in Spain,
    If you read them one day once a week,
        You'll have six nights of nightmare.

A DREAM

I STOOD alone in a silent town,
  The moon shone sharp and bright
On a row of dead, who paced along
  In sad and weary plight,
Bearing their tombstones back and front.
  Like sandwich-men at night.

I read the epitaphs in front,
  They'd all been good and kind.
They all were men of sterling worth,
  And qualities of mind ;
But a hand of fire had traced the truth
  On the stone that hung behind.

Their eyes were fixed on the words of fire
  That blazed on the next one's stone,
And each was chaunting his neighbour's sin

D

In a grumbling undertone ;
While his heart was wrung, his ears were racked,
As he listened to his own.

Anon there passed me another row,
  And these were women-kind ;
Their faults were on the stone in front,
  Their virtues hung behind ;
Each woman was chaunting a woman's praise,
  But to her faults was blind.

Unequal was their lot on earth,
  But equal in Death's holding,
For man would feel as sharp a pain
  Another's faults unfolding,
As that a woman's heart would know
  Forbid another's scolding.

THE DEATH OF DAY

Day was dying an infant's death,
    Softly sleeping.
Evening caught her latest breath,
    Stilly weeping
Over the hills, the lost one's bier,
    Tears of dew ;
Night with dark hand slowly drew,
    Drew more near,
Over the colourless woods a shroud,
A dull gray fold of hueless cloud,
While the old owls hoot from the ivy nigh,
Bid the mourner's torches thronging the sky
Pass in silent procession by.

THE MISTRAL AND THE PALMS

The mistral leapt from his mountain lair,
 From his coverlet of snow,
He silvered the olive groves above,
 He whitened the bay below,
With his raiment he roughly wrested off
 As the noon's hot sun did glow.

The palm trees shivered, and bent their heads
 As he rushed triumphant by,
Then flung their leaves to the blue o'erhead,
 That blazed like an eastern sky,
They felt they had left their fatherland
 Like the invalids   to die.

HE AND SHE

HE

Love lies sleeping,
Cradled, dimpling
Smiles are rimpling
Little cheeks that know not weeping :
Little lips that know not lying,
Petal-puckered, look, are trying
    For breast kisses,
    Little blisses
Safe within the mother's keeping —
    Shall we wake him,
      You and I ?

SHE

Love is flushing
Dreaming, wooing
Our undoing ;
Cheeks will learn the need of blushing,
Lips will learn the art of scolding,
Cruel thoughts in words unfolding ;
He may tease us,
And displease us,
Past the power of mother's hushing
E'er we wake him,
Friend, good-bye !

A PRAYER

NATURE, fickle, frugal jade !
Wasteth nought that she has made ;
  She hath store-house up above,
  Whither failures are respited,
    Else where goeth all the love
    Unreturned and unrequited?

Nature, if this may be so,
There's a little maid I know,
  Lacking in her love of me ;
  From your store her breast imbueing.
    She will yearn, and there shall be
    Half the trouble saved of wooing.

LOVE'S LANGUAGE

Tongues may talk treason,
　And lips may lisp lies,
Learn in love's season
　The language of eyes.

To-morrow they know not,
　They live for to-day ;
Love glances show not
　If it's earnest or play.

Seek but eyes' answers
　When love calls the tune,
Twined like two dancers
　Revolving as one.

If eyes be demurring,
　Try pressure of hands,
An instinct unerring
　The touch understands.

Love's eloquence truthful
    Lives an hour or a day:
A heart that is youthful
    Delights in his play.

Such sweet conversation
    Ends if there's no slip,
In a long peroration
    Of lip upon lip.

AT THE SIGN OF THE REMBRANDT HEAD

MAIDEN, now with a love-look lither,
   Now as made marble statuesque,
Is 't Art or Love that brings you hither?
   Art erotic, Love Rembrandtesque?

Say, did Mercury Hail him thither,
   Or Cupid?   He bows with feigned surprise ;
Arcades ambo ! I fear that neither
   The man nor the maid seem overwise.

Art may be long, but Love is fleeting,
   Play with him e'er he be lost or dead,
Was it not this your message of meeting,
   ' Noon at the sign of the Rembrandt Head ? '

A LESSON IN LOVE

There may come a day
My dearie,
Love will fly away,
Aweary
Will be our nights without him, our days be long and
dreary.

Roses shed their bloom
Around us ;
'Twas the roses' doom
To mound us
Deep in scented death of flower where none but Love
had found us.

' Follow me,' sang Love :
' The roses
Perish, and thereof
The posies
Will but be your funeral wreaths when youth's rose
season closes.'

Hand in hand we went,
  Love leading,
Sweet the hours we spent,
  Unheeding
A vision of a leafless rose and two torn hearts a-bleeding.

Follow Love too far,
  He'll weary,
Rest we where we are,
  My dearie,
Lest the poise of tiring wings rebear him to his eerie.

AFTER PARTING

WE parted, vowed to meet no more,
Locked love behind your conscience door,
Set resolution's guard before.

Deeply I drank dream-potioned sleep,
What helps it vigil vain to keep,
When to be wakeful is to weep?

When all the looks and words of years,
Remembered now in idle fears,
Fall multiplied in falling tears?

I woke and cursed the risen sun
That he had all too soon begun
The day on which my love was done.

But, as the sun rose, the wind sped,
And shook the dews the night had shed
From every fresh-blown flowerhead.

Like light-lit meadows after rain,
All my old love grew green again,
Pleasure more sweet for passing pain.

I met you at the garden gate ;
' Too soon,' you cried, ' or else too late
To alter : kiss me, it is fate.'

*TOO LATE TO CALL BACK YESTERDAY,
AND TO-MORROW COMES NOT YET.*

COME back, dead hours of yesterday,
To-day I hate,
To-morrow comes not, vain to pray,
We cannot turn on life's highway
Or alter fate.

We cannot pause, and bid the moon
We watched together,
Stand still in vale of Ajalon,
In memory of that afternoon
Amid the heather.

How bright she sailed above the firs
When evening fell,
Your sweet sad face was pale as hers,
My heart was beating with desires
I dared not tell.

But e'er we reached the wicket-gate,
　　I think you knew
The kindly touch of courted fate
Had kindled pure yet passionate
　　My love for you.

Come back, dead hours of yesterday;
　　The moon to-night
Shall touch me with remembering ray,
Sha'l bid my dreams in fancy play
　　With past delight.

RELEASE

WE kissed amid the bracken—
　If Love were only true,
The silver cord might slacken
　　But Love, alas ! is deathful,
　　No lover ever faithful
　If Love were only true,
The golden sun should blacken
　Ere I would part from you.

My darling, we should rue it
　If life were ever young,
A few sweet springs undo it.
　　The deed that we have done,
　　The kiss that made us one—
　If life were ever young,
No autumn to bedew it,
　　Our hearts would soon be wrung.

My love, there is no telling,
  If Death would only show
The secrets of his dwelling,
    That we might not believe it
    Were best for us to leave it-
  If Death would only show,
His was the gift of healing,
    This life of love—and woe.

ONE SUMMER NIGHT

THE summer night was faint, close overhead
The stars hung, from the depths illimited
    Of the black pool below they gazed at me.
Seeming the wistful eyes of all the dead.

A black fish moved, behind him the weeds waved,
Like long hands beckoning me : the bright eyes braved
    Me plunge and join the silence, join with thee
My other self in the still deep engraved.

My watch was ticking loud time's passing feet,
My heart was marking life's way with its beat.
    And nothing else seemed in the world alive,
Swooned in the utterness of summer heat.

While ever from the silence of the pool
The eyes said ' Coward,' twinkled at me ' Fool,
    To-morrow will not yesterday forgive ;
Plunge, here is rest, the grave is quiet and cool.'

But suddenly upleapt a little wind,
The fir-top whispered and the rush inclined,
   The black sky palpitated into white,
Till those appealing eyes were stricken blind,

As silently behind the hill uprolled
The glorious moon from the sun's bath of gold,
   Which flowed from her, and left her wondrous bright,
Silvering the wood and whitening the wold.

Passed was the need of death, the thoughts of gloom,
Like Lazar's cerecloths at the opened tomb.
   They fell from me, and as I faced the light
All life seemed odorous with a new perfume.

To-morrow shall sad yesterday forget,
That sudden shaft of moon its amulet,
   And all the mellowed marvels of to-night
Illuminate the sadness of regret.

CONTRARINESS

I PRAYED and prayed for my heart's desire,
  At morning and eventide,
The gods were deaf to my words of fire,
And left me unsatisfied.

Desire may wither, the gods may tire,
  The gods had tired, desire had died,
As soon as a new love rose to admire,
  My old love was by my side.

THE PITY OF IT

WHILE our early years are spent
In a childish discontent
That we are not born grown up —
What a pity there's no hope
Of our finding later joys
Half so unalloyed as toys !

When we love, as love we must,
In a woman place our trust,
Try to cage the passing wind —
What a pity Love is blind,
Blind and dumb, and will not tell
He leadeth to the gates of Hell !

When ambition fires our breast,
When we saddle for the quest
Of riches, power, knowledge, fame —

What a pity that the game
Has so very, very few
Prizes worth the waste of thew !

When in age we faint and fall,
Turn our faces to the wall,
Knowledge of our life complete—
What a pity 'tis too late !
Had we known we might have spent
Half our days in quiet content.

A STORM

Look up, my heart ! See the storm without,
    How the dim trees with their mystic hands
        Catch at the splatters of rain.
Hark ! How the wet wind's strangled shout,
    Full of the torture of silent lands,
        Dies away in a wail of pain.

Look up, my heart ! See that flash of fire ;
    Hark to the rolling rush of its wings,
        Like the flame of Love in my soul !
Shall it sear thee, heart, with a hot desire,
    Till it sever the cord of the silver strings,
        Till it shatter the golden bowl ?

No ; for see, my heart, the rush of the rain,
    And the burst of the lightning's power,
        Has fled as the dark has fled,

And the spirit of storm in vain
   Has ridden in might for an hour,
      For the night of his power is dead.

Look up, my heart ! Thy passionate love
   Shall waste with the waste of a night
      At the rise of a kindlier day ;
Little the trace of the ravage thereof,
   And the dawn awaits with a purer light
      The next love that comes thy way.

WILD OR TAME

Through paths of a wood unweeded,
  O'er green of a meadow unmown,
  I follow my rose, my own,
Where the rich ripe grass has seeded,
  The sower of tares has sown.

Though yesterday's free wild flowers
  Have died in the drought of to-day,
  Fresh blooms spring up by the way,
And the shaded banks of the hours
  Are fertile in love's highway.

The songs of the wild bird harden,
  Their beauty grows less and less,
  In a builded wilderness,
The cultured grace of the garden
  Lacks the wild bank's loveliness.

Society seeking station
    Courts love for the gold it brings,
    The bright bait whirls and sings,
Till an aching heart's oblation
    On a hollow altar rings.

But still there's a garden of beauties,
    Where the richest and rarest are sown,
    There blows my rose, my own,
Where purest in flavour the fruit is,
    Though the sower of tares has sown.

MEMORY

WOULD'ST thou drink of memory's cup?
    Hold it lightly, and beware
Lest thou rashly stirrest up
    The rank lees of poison there.

Sip the froth upon the brim,
    Loves and pleasures lightly rise,
Sparkling to the crystal rim,
    All that's painful deeper lies.

When thou feelest thou are toiled
    In the quicksands of old age,
That the sport of life is spoiled
    In disease's vassalage,

Take the cup and gaze therein,
    Thou hast mixed it drop by drop,
With worth and work or shame and sin
    Thou hast slowly filled it up.

With the froth thy lips are wet,
    Dash it from thee and be free,
Or drain it to the dregs, and let
    Thy ill deeds poison thee.

DAWN AND EVE

At the summons of the sun,
  How the birds are singing,
Where the gossamer has spun,
  Their little loves are winging.
As boys and maidens laughing run,
  To youth's young pleasures clinging.

In the quiet evening time,
  At the still sunsetting
How the gnats beneath the lime
  In mazy darts are fretting,
Like memories of youthful prime
  When age begins forgetting.

A LESSON

The dahlias frost-emblackened drooped.
  With rime their leaves were wet,
You turned your mock on them, and stooped
  To pluck a violet ;
Then lightly turning, laughed and looped
  My heart within your net.

You taught me to forget the past
  With the living flower you gave,
To learn that nothing 's born to last,
  And little meant to save—
My love is on another cast
  Now you are in your grave.

A WOMAN'S FRIENDSHIP

This morning arm in arm enlaced,
  We wandered where the garden ends,
Our eyes, lips, thoughts, our hearts embraced,
  And every gossip knew us friends -
    To-night you call me ' traitor, thief,'
    And gladden as you give me grief.

Our joys, our tears, our lives we've shared,
  My girlhood's homage all you took—
I sought him not—I should be spared
  Your hot reproach, your chilly look—
    ' Love, Sweet,' you called me—by his side
    Sitting, I saw your lips had lied.

A stranger, he was nought to me--
  But, were love perfect, how should fear
Endanger friendship's constancy?

Fear lest a man should prove more dear ;
I had been gladdened if I knew
He loved you, for his choice of you.

.

'Tis time we parted. I have known
A woman's friendship, lightly lost
For little, but I feel my own
Is sacrificed at cruel cost.
Too long I've been your friend, your slave,
' Thief ! traitor !' take the words you gave.

KISMET !

From England wedding-bells
  Sound the seas over,
Thither, where dreaming dwells
  Her absent lover.
          Kismet ! Kismet !

Death, art thou pitiless ?
  War flags are flying,
Many who sought thee less
  Round him are dying.
          Kismet ! Kismet !

In England once again
  They meet in sadness ;
Love, break the ring in twain,
  Save him from madness.
          Kismet ! Kismet !

EARTH AND SEA

THEIR loves are eternal,
Their kisses diurnal,
  And, faithfully free,
  The earth and the sea
    Commingle their tresses
      Where'er his waves range,
    In endless caresses
      Of infinite change.

Though to-day he be chiding
And angrily hiding
  'Neath storm cloud and hail,
  He will ripple a tale
    Of repentance to-morrow,
      Will daintily toy
    With her teardrops of sorrow,
      And turn them to joy.

How bold he advances,
How bright the light dances
　In the blue of his eyes ;
　Till, wet with surprise,
　　Her lashes discover
　　　"Twixt the salt and the sown
　　The lips of her lover
　　　Laid cool on her own.

How gentle the wooing,
From ebbing to flowing ;
　The gentler retreat
　From her lips to her feet,
　　Is a lover's manœuvre,
　　　"Twixt a kiss and a kiss,
　　To please her and prove her
　　　All fair and all his.

AUTUMN

BRIGHT, white, the October sun
Burneth at noon, embossed upon the blue,
   Winter's cold hands upon
His setting, chill above the risen dew
   He riseth, mists forerun
Him as he comes to bid the leaves adieu.

   They drank his early fires —
How long it seems back to the gladdening spring,
   When first the larches' spires
Of emerald waved like a bee-eater's wing
   The leaves' outburnt desires
Already fear stern winter's reckoning.

   The growing ground is swept
Of flower and fruit and corn ; the naked vine,
   The gathered orchard kept

But little time their ripeness, while supine
      Upon the harvest slept
Soft summer, recking not the spent sunshine.

    The moist soil peels aside
As the share goes 'neath where the ripe corn stood,
    The darkening pines divide
The rustling russets of the dying wood ;
    From hill to garden side
Earth mourneth beautiful in widowhood.

    Night groweth strong, his head
Brilliant with frosty stars ; brief yesterday
    To his Procrustes bed
He shortens, clips the wings of her ; To-day
    With darkness overshed
Closes her houred pinions in dismay.

'*HOSIA PANOURGEIN*'

' MURDER thou shalt not commit,'
  God's hest is over us all—
Pardon. The beacon is lit,
  Country, I list to thy call.

Broadbrim may turn up his eyes,
  Insult, invite, and retreat—
Nobler the freeman who dies,
  Brooking not slur or defeat.

Easy to sit and to spin,
  Soften in cowardly ease—
While there are battles to win,
  Spread the old flag to the breeze.

Sweet are the blessings of peace,
  Loved is the landscape of home—
While there are wrongs to redress
  Ours be the fight and the foam.

OFF FINISTERRE

THE storm wind rose in sudden wrath,
 His ermine robe tore he,
Then hurled the snowy fragments forth
 Upon the sabled sea,
Whose wild waves swelled from South to North
 And ragéd furiously.

Like racing giants with clenching grip,
 They thundered the Bay along,
They threatened to rend the rocks, and rip
 The timbers staunch and strong—
The wave whose lip shall swallow the ship
 To him shall the prize belong.

TO AN OLD OAK

A THOUSAND years since some chance acorn sowing
Engendered thee amid thy forest peers,
Now gnarled and hollow with the pain of growing
    A thousand years.
Life's joys decay as vigour disappears :
Dost not regret the time when, ripe for throwing,
The axe-stroke passed thee ?   All the many spears

Of grass are happier, who at summer mowing
Fall in full-flowered beauty.   Mourner's tears
Are vain o'er manhood's tomb, dead without knowing
    Thy thousand years.

FROST

I AM southing, and before me
    Souths the swallow,
    As I follow
From the hardy North who bore me,
    Hill and hollow,
Mere and meadow, still and stormy,
With a silent worship stricken, stiffened into ice, adore
  me.

I am bringing to the garden
    Sleep and leisure,
    Foolish pleasure
Lays aside her gaudy burden,
    As the measure
Song-birds sing doth cease, and harden
All the flippant buds a-sparkle with pure jewels of my
  treasure.

I the bridegroom am, beside me,
    Dainty, surely,
    Soft, demurely,
Steals my snow bride : safe abide we
    Loving purely,
Till the cruel sun shall chide me—
Then she'll melt into my arms, and I in earth's recesses
    hide me.

SUMMER DAWN

O ! PURE is the summer sunrise hour,
  In the star of the morning's keeping,
The evil spirits have lost their power,
  And even lust lies sleeping.
    Trade and politics cease their lying—
    Only awake the watchers, the dying,
  Or the homeless outcast weeping.

The past returns in the scent of dreams,
  To the widow her wedding gladness,
To the lover the love that is lost, the gleams
  Of gold to the pauper, and all the sadness
    Of age is lost in the hopes of youth,
    Renewed in slumber, when dreams seem truth
  And only waking madness.

ON EXMOOR

He who hath seen the antlered monarch weep,
Bayed where he soils in Barle or Exe's sweep,
   When, royal heart, he faces hound and man,
Though royal limbs have failed to brave the steep

Beyond the river, where the mild-eyed hinds
Await him, feels that something blinds
   His own eyes too, and half the autumn light
Has left the landscape where the water winds.

THE FIVE SENSES

A cosy room in a quiet street,
A London sybarite's retreat,
A ring of the bell, a step on the stair,
A tap at the panel and she is there.

He was dreaming how but a year ago
She stood where the garden roses blow,
And how like a startled roe-deer shy
Young love leapt out from eye to eye.

He was hearing again as last year he heard
Her love confessed in a whispered word,
Knowing her lips would re-echo soon
The old, fond, well-remembered tune.

He was thinking of that pure garden scent
That faded away as the summer went,
And now a subtler, rarer perfume,
The incense of passion, pervades his room.

The ripe fruits' savour of yesteryear
Comes back as he feels her presence near ;
Ripe fruits are plucked, ripe lips are kissed,
Arcadian innocence hardly missed.

A pressure of hands, a close embrace,
Speechless they stand there face to face,
While their throbbing touch and their eyes reveal
The passion that two young lovers feel.

Each sense inveigles in early days
Of wandering down a new love's ways,
When once the maiden is wooed and won
The senses five are merged in one.

MY SHADOW AND I

I ASKED my shadow one summer day
   Whither he went when the light had fled :
He blushed quite dark in a shadowy way,
   ' I go nowhither, my lord,' he said.

' Shadow, thou liest,' then bending I
   Laid me adown on the growing grass,
My back to the ground, my face to the sky,
   No eye could see where my shadow was.

' Henchman, thou lovest the light of the sun,
   Lovest to wave o'er the wild flowers' hue,
What is it thou hast in the darkness done ?
   Answer me truth and I'll walk with you.'

Then up I arose, and a rustle o'erwent
   The crushed wild flowers as the laid grass stood,
For they felt that my shadow's punishment
   Was heavy on their little lustihood.

' Master, when slumber unfetters me, mine
  To leave you leaveless and wander far,
To the silent garden of Proserpine,
  Where living shadows and dead men are.

' There till I a patch of grey garden ground,
  I plant the thoughts you have thought awake,
Gracious and gruesome their hues confound,
  Not a bloom of them all shall wither or shake.

' There come the shadows of loves outworn,
  To gaze on the flowers they sowed in your breast.
And many a one departs less forlorn
  When her rose-bud has whispered " I love you best." '

IN AN ALBUM

'Come hither, come hither, my pages twain,
  You of the sad and sober e'e,
  And you of the comic brain,
    One of you gay as a weather-cock,
    The other grave as the nether rock,
      Come hither, and quickly together knock,
        Lines for a faire ladye.'

'My master, it liketh me not this task,
  Many a mood hath a ladye faire,
An' if she be merry she will but ask
    How so grave a varlet approach her dare—
      No errands to ladies for me—
        Two sen'night hence,
        On no pretence
      Will I take further guerdon of thee.'

' So I say, master, maybe her lips
    Will be quivering still with passion or grief,
She will but scorn my frolicksome quips,
    And treat me worse than a tramping thief—
        No errands to ladies for me—
            I give you warning
            O' the thirtieth morning
        To pay my last wages to me.'

'Get hence, get hence, my pages twain,
    You of the gay and festive e'e,
And you of the sober brain,
    Quick to the right about,
    Forth from my sight get out,
    I will now write about
        You to the faire ladye.'

TO HER THIMBLE

ROUND and rough and dented in,
  Hast thou seen a battle?
Hast thou felt the prick of pin,
  Heard the needles rattle?
Was thou as an helmet meant
  For some sturdy dwarf? or
A Liliputian's tiny tent
  In some puny warfare?
No, thine was a gentler trade,
  Finger-tip protector,
Thou didst shield a winsome maid,
  Cunning dress dissector.
Dost thou mourn thy mistress lost,
  Miss her motions nimble,
As the work was lightly tossed,
  Melancholy thimble?

' Did I know those fairy fingers ? '
  What insinuation !
Saucy thimble, yet there lingers
  In thy touch temptation.

'EROS ANIKATE MACHAN'

(From the 'Antigone')

STROPHE

O ! LOVE, undefeated,
As conqueror greeted,
   From battle to battle,
   O maker of slaves !
Now rustic, now viking,
Thou wanderest liking,
   Now shepherds' snug wattles,
   Now surging sea waves.
Thou slumberest often
Where maiden's cheeks soften,
   Her blushes endrape thee –
   Can ephemeral man
Avoid thee by flying?
When e'en th' undying
   Ones cannot escape thee—
   Sure madness thy ban.

ANTISTROPHE

The righteous thou wrestest
Awry, and molestest
  Their hearts to their ruin,
    Thou makest them sin.
'Tis thou, hardest hearted,
That hast cruelly started
  This fatal death doing
    'Twixt kinsmen and kin.
Desire fondly beaming
From eyes that are gleaming
  With love for the plighted
    Shows the struggle is won ;
Desire sits anointed
'Side divine laws appointed,
  While sports, unaffrighted,
    Aphrodite, alone.

THE WINE SHOP

(From François Coppée)

A DRUNKARD sat drowning the dreams he hated
Deep in the wine cup, unsubjugated
By the flies in the hot sun congregated—
    He was one whom despair excuses.

While he mouthingly moved his wet lips about,
Like a stall-stuffed ox, the decanter stout
Had tumbled, and just like a hiccupping spout,
    On the table the wine diffuses.

O! the whirling weight in the aching head,
Leant on the hands while disorderéd
Thoughts are swinging like dinging lead
    In a deep bell telling our shame.

Something dramatic I thought must be there ;
I approached, and with weary fingers, where
The wine had sputtered, with drunken care
    He was tracing a woman's name.

AN ANSWER

(*From François Coppée*)

' I HAVE seen him but so little,' you said the other day :
I answer, have I known any more of yours and you?
In a moment my whole heart resigned without ado,
Cannot you return my love in the same sweet sudden
    way?

For to mount the highest tower at one strong wing-essay,
To fire the stormy distance with flashing clear-lit hue,
To enchant with potent mirage no mortal can eschew,
Does't take the eagle, lightning, love, a moment or a
    day?

'Tis true I hardly saw you, but was ravished, love, and I
To deserve you gladly consecrate my life until I die,
And all to-morrow's sombre threats right willingly defy.

It cannot be that mutual love a longer friendship claims,
Since to enkindle all my breast and set my heart in flames,
Dear love, one single glance sufficed, one spark fallen
from your eye.

FROM HEINE

Lay your dainty fingers, darling,
  On my heart and hearken,
How within its tiny chamber
    There's a rap, rap, rapping ;
    It is a cunning carpenter,
  My coffin he is tapping,
  All my rest kidnapping :
Daily, nightly, doth he keep
  Knock, knock, knocking
    O haste thee, Master Carpenter,
I fain would fall on sleep.

Spottiswoode & Co. Printers, New-street Square, London.

www.ingramcontent.com/pod-product-compliance
Lightning Source LLC
Chambersburg PA
CBHW060246030726
47493CB00025B/2750

* 9 7 8 3 3 3 7 2 6 0 9 6 5 *